Giraffe Trouble

by Jean Craighead George

Illustrated by Anna Vojtech

Disney PRESS

New York

A lioness roared from the lake shore when Cam was born.

The calf's stately mother paid no attention. She was a big and powerful giraffe. She could protect Cam with her long legs and sharp hooves. She could knock down a lion or a hyena.

And she was protected by friends. Four alert mother giraffes were in the woods guarding the giraffe nursery where their calves and Cam lay. The mothers watched for lions and hyenas, cheetahs and angry hippos. When they went out to browse, the giraffe fathers stood guard.

Cam was six feet tall at birth. No sooner had her mother licked her dry with her eighteen-inch-long tongue than Cam got to her feet and nursed. A few hours later she stepped out of the nursery to look at the world. Cam was utterly fearless. This worried her mother. Fearless calves often do not grow up. They need to be wise as well.

It was early morning when Cam stepped out onto the savanna. The rainy season had just begun. The grasses were a fresh spring-green. Herds of zebras, gazelles, and wildebeests grazed all the way to the mountains. Thousands of them fed on the grasses.

Not her family. The long-necked giraffes found their meals high above everyone else. They relished the leaves of the trees. The big bulls could reach up more than nineteen feet.

Cam's family wandered in a loose herd from woodland to woodland. They had no special territory. Adults and young all moved along amicably, finding their own trees and keeping several giraffe lengths apart. Old bulls, like Cam's grandfather Elo, preferred to live alone.

Giraffes are sweet and peaceful animals. They are also very smart. They see trouble and avoid it. Cam's herd drank at the rhino wallow, not the lake where the lions lived. Lions attack young giraffes.

Fortunately, after she had seen the vast savanna, fearless Cam stayed close to her mother. At least she did so for three months. Then she developed a craving for the buds of the combretum trees that grew along the lake.

One day when her mother was eating acacia leaves, Cam smelled the tasty combretum. Fearlessly she strode off to find them. She walked past the lion pride. The lioness opened one eye. She did not stalk Cam. Even a little giraffe can kick hard. She would wait until Cam lay down to chew her cud and rest.

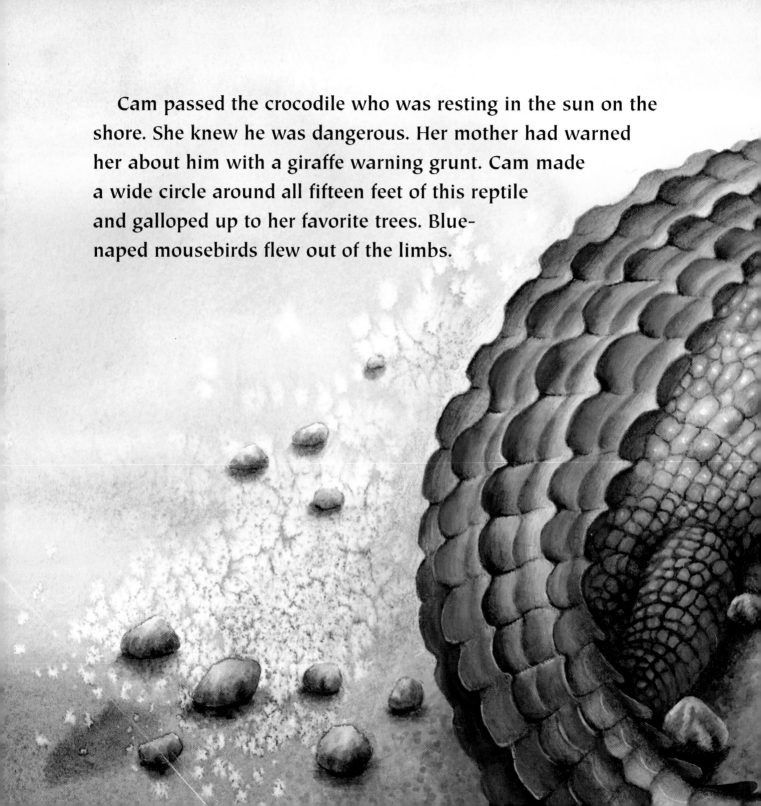

Cam passed the crocodile who was resting in the sun on the shore. She knew he was dangerous. Her mother had warned her about him with a giraffe warning grunt. Cam made a wide circle around all fifteen feet of this reptile and galloped up to her favorite trees. Blue-naped mousebirds flew out of the limbs.

She lifted her long muzzle into the tasty leaves and tore them off with her flexible upper lip. Her long tongue reached out and whipped the leaves into her mouth. She ate and ate.

When she was stuffed, she walked to a patch of grass. Cam got down on her front knees, then her back knees, and finally rolled comfortably onto her side. She lay perfectly still. The croc did not see her, for crocs see only things that move.

But the lioness saw Cam. She lifted her head. The calf was an easy meal. She was lying down. The lioness got to her feet.

She took to the rain-dampened grasses. They did not rustle when she walked through them like dry grasses do. In utter silence, she stalked Cam.

Along the lake lived a community of sharp-eyed birds. The flamingos saw the lioness. As one, they all stopped swinging their beaks in the muddy backwater and stretched up their necks.

"*Ka-baunk.*" They screamed out the flamingo alarm cry. Cam opened her eyes.

The cry alerted the ducks. They, too, saw the lioness, honked, and took to the air. Cam lifted her long neck and head.

The ducks alerted a flock of Egyptian geese.
Wind from their big wings bent the grasses. As
they flew off, Cam saw the lioness.

It took mere seconds to lift her rear end, get to
her front knees, and stand up. That was too long.
The lioness was in the air coming toward her like
a missile.

Out of nowhere came Elo, the old bull giraffe. He slashed down on the lioness with his razor-sharp hooves. The lioness rolled into the dust, gained her feet, and sped away. The old bull sounded the raucous cough of the victorious male.

Cam galloped back to the nursery. Her mother greeted her by curling her long lip over Cam's nose. She did not scold Cam. Wise youngsters of the wild learn from mistakes.

Cam was now both fearless and wise. Her mother gently rubbed her head against Cam's. Her calf would grow up after all.

Cast of Characters

RETICULATED GIRAFFE
Cam
scientific name: *Giraffa camelopardalis reticulata*

The giraffe is the tallest mammal in the world, easily recognized by its long, long legs and neck. When they are three years old, males leave their mothers and join bachelor herds. The males have a medium horn and four or more bumps for fighting contests. One young is born after a gestation of fourteen to fifteen months.

LION
King of the African Carnivores
Cam's enemy
scientific name: *Panthera leo*

A large robust cat with smooth tawny coat and a long tail with a black tassel at tip. The male develops a blond, tawny, or even black mane in his third year. One to four, rarely five or six, cubs are born after a 3.5-month gestation. The cubs have brownish spots that fade around three months of age.

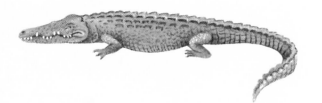

LONG-SNOUTED CROCODILE
Cam's lake edge enemy
scientific name: *Crocodylus cataphractus*

Crocodiles are large, lizardlike animals with powerful jaws, many teeth, short legs, and webbed toes. The ancestors of the crocodile lived at the same time as the dinosaurs. Of the world's twenty-three species, most are endangered. They eat fish, but will ambush antelopes, buffaloes, zebras, and domestic animals that come to their waterways to drink. They lay thirteen to twenty-seven eggs in a mound of vegetable debris, which warms the eggs as it decays.

EGYPTIAN GOOSE
Cam's water friend
scientific name: *Alopochen aegyptacus*

This large, pale gray and brown goose with white shoulders wears dark rings around its eyes. No other large waterfowl has these. It mates for life and nests on the ground or in tree holes.

FLAMINGO
Cam's friend who warns her of danger
scientific name: *Phoenicopterus ruber*

The flamingo is a huge, white or pale pink bird with a long S-shaped neck. It builds a tall mud nest in which it makes a depression for one egg. When feeding it walks steadily in water keeping its head submerged for up to twenty-five seconds. It stirs up the bottom mud with its feet and filters out tiny water life from the mud.

ZEBRA
Cam's savanna neighbor
scientific name: *Equus burchelli*

The zebra resembles a sturdy pony, decorated with handsome black or brown stripes that distinguish it from all other beasts. A male weighs about 550 pounds, the female about 480. Females give birth to one foal after a twelve month gestation.

WILDEBEEST
Brindled Gnu
Cam's savanna neighbor
scientific name: *Connochaetes taurinus*

A wildebeest is an unusual-looking antelope with flat muzzle, cow-like horns, and short neck. It is blue-gray or brown. It weighs 350 to 600 pounds. One calf is born after a gestation of eight to eight-and-a-half months. It migrates in huge herds on the savanna.

Disney is committed to wildlife conservation world-wide. At Disney's Animal Kingdom, most of the animals that guests will see were born in zoological parks. A safari adventure ride features live animals in a re-creation of the African savanna. Guests can also visit Conservation Station, the headquarters for conservation and species survival activities.

CONSERVATION
STATION

AFRICA

CONSERVATION
TRAIN STATION

ASIA
(To open early
1999)

GORILLA FALLS
EXPLORATION
TRAIL

AFRICA
TRAIN STATION

DISCOVERY RIVER

TREE OF LIFE

SAFARI VILLAGE

OASIS

DINOLAND U.S.A.

ENTRANCE

DISNEY'S
ANIMAL
KINGDOM

To Kate
—J.C.G.

To Franciska and Johanna
—A.V.

Text © 1998 by Jean Craighead George.
Illustrations © 1998 by Anna Vojtech.

Printed in the United States of America.
The text for this book is set in 16-point Tiepolo Bold. The artwork for
each picture was painted with watercolors.

First Edition
1 3 5 7 9 10 8 6 4 2

Library of Congress Cataloging-in-Publication Data
George, Jean Craighead, (date)
Giraffe trouble / by Jean Craighead George; illustrated by Anna Vojtech.
—1st ed.
p.   cm.
Summary: A young giraffe living on the African plains learns how to be
wise as well as fearless when a lion attacks.
ISBN 0-7868-3167-7 (trade)—0-7868-5066-3 (lib. bdg.)
1. Giraffe—Juvenile fiction.   [1. Giraffe—Fiction.]
I. Vojtech, Anna, ill.   II. Title.
PZ10.3.G316Gi   1998
[E]—dc21   97-33130